THE IRISH GRAVE

RAVEN HILL FARM MYSTERIES

BOOK FOUR

JANE E. DREW

JANE DREW PUBLISHING, LLC.

CHAPTER 1

"Why have we never thought of getting a cat before?" Fiona Fitzsimmons sat cradling a kitten in her lap that looked to be about three months old. It was a calico with an orange back, white legs, and chest. "Shouldn't every farm have a cat? I mean, there are mice and rats to contend with. So it just makes perfect sense to me."

Quinn had to laugh. "You don't have to sell me on that kitten, Fiona. Whoever left it at our front door knew what they were doing. I'm already in love with the little thing. I wonder, though, how do you tell if it's a boy or a girl?"

"Hmm, no idea. I know; let's ask Margaret!" Said Fiona.

Margaret O'Callahan had been their go-to on almost everything since the two women had pulled up their Chicago roots and moved to a little farm in West Cork near Ballyfrannen. Margaret and her brother Daniel had been their first friends in Ireland. Daniel had even entrusted Quinn with the Raven he had rescued. Pike had become a part of the family. He lived in the house and came and went as he pleased. Both she and Fiona loved the bird dearly.

Margaret and Daniel had also come to their rescue when

they bought two Sandy and Black pigs from a breeder in the UK, patiently teaching them how to care for the creatures. The same was true when they added the chickens and their recent purchase of two miniature donkeys. Quinn and Fiona were thankful to have them in their lives. Fiona was incredibly grateful to have met Daniel. She was, in fact, secretly in love with him.

The following day, Margaret stopped by with a basket of baked goods left over from breakfast at her B&B. Margaret was round, with a quick walk, and thick, wiry red hair that seemed to hover above her head no matter how many times she tried to push it down. She was a woman who was always ready to speak her mind but also had a kind heart and a wicked sense of humor. This morning, Margaret had brought bread pudding with nutmeg, a few slices of butterscotch apple cake, and an assortment of scones.

"Yum," said Fiona, lifting a slice of apple cake from the basket and putting it on her plate.

Quinn chose a blueberry scone as Fiona placed a large pot of tea, cups, and saucers on their well-used pine kitchen table. The women were ready to tuck in when a light tap at the back door told them Hattie Biggs had walked the short distance from her cottage next door to join them. This ritual played out at least twice a week, sometimes more. The women liked nothing better than these morning gatherings.

Hattie was in her early fifties, tall and thin, with her hair pulled back rather severely and no makeup. Her dress of choice was a wool jumper, a tweed skirt, and no-nonsense shoes. That's how Hattie chose to look unless it wasn't.

Hattie had been one of her day's most successful and beautiful models. Back then, she had used the name Antonia. Now, when it suited her, she could still transform into an older version of the beautiful creature she was. But, mostly, she enjoyed being plain Hattie Biggs.

Fiona sighed as she finished the last bite of the large slice of butterscotch apple cake. "Good god, Margaret, that was delicious!"

Margaret smiled. "My mam has been baking that since I was a wee lass. It's one of my favorites, too. Would ye like another piece, Fee?"

"I'd better not, Margaret, though there is something you can help me with." Fiona looked around the kitchen for the kitten. It was curled up, sleeping next to Maggie, Quinn's Border Terrier. Fee brought the kitten to Margaret. "Someone left this little thing outside our front door. Maybe you can tell us if it's a boy or a girl?" The kitten gave a soft meow as Margaret gently turned it upside down for an inspection.

"Well, you're a little fella, aren't you?" Margaret righted the kitten and began stroking its back. It immediately settled into her lap, purring.

"It's a boy, then?" From Fiona.

"It is indeed." Margaret continued to stroke the kitten. "Do you have a name for him yet?"

"I thought Binx would be a nice name. What do you think, Quinn?" Fiona looked at her friend of many years to get her reaction.

"Binx, yes, that has a nice ring to it."

"Binx it is then." Fiona looked at the kitten and smiled.

Just then, the women heard a knock at the front door. Quinn looked out to see Dermot Brennan standing on the front stoop. Dermot was the local Garda from Ballyfrannen, the little town Quinn and Fiona had fallen in love with and the reason they had moved to this part of County Cork.

"Hello, Dermot; what brings you out on this fine, sunny day?" Quinn had a history with Dermot. At first glance, he appeared to be nothing more than a small, nervous man who seemed in constant motion, bobbing up and down and smoothing his oversized jacket. There was much more to him, though, as Quinn had learned. Dermot was a master of jujitsu and quite capable of being a commanding presence when the occasion called for it. He had more than earned Quinn's respect many times over and had even saved her life once.

"Well, Missus, I thought I might come in and chat if you don't mind. There's some news I thought you would want to hear about." Dermot sniffed and looked a little uneasy as he heard voices and laughter from the kitchen.

"Oh, that's just Hattie and Margaret. Join us for some tea while you tell us the news. Margaret has brought over some delicious leftovers." Quinn ushered Dermot into the kitchen.

Dermot laughed nervously and pulled at his jacket. "Are you sure you ladies don't mind me interrupting you like this? I can always come back later." Dermot sniffed again and smoothed his hair down as he spoke. "Honestly, coming back later is no trouble at all." Dermot looked back towards the living room and the front door.

Margaret slammed her hand on the table, causing Dermot to jump violently. "Jesus god, Dermot, stop your swanning about. Sit down here and have some tea." Margaret pointed to the chair next to her. She got up to get a cup and saucer and plate and fork. She sat those items down before Dermot, who looked a little wild-eyed. "Now, so, what would ye be havin'? And don't say nothin', as you've no meat on your bones as it is." Margaret waited for Dermot to respond.

Dermot tentatively reached for a piece of the butterscotch apple cake. He seemed to relax a little as Margaret poured him some tea and then sat back down. "Well, this is a treat. I should stop by and see you and Fiona more often." Dermot chuckled and looked at Quinn as he spoke.

"You're welcome anytime," replied Quinn, "but you said there was some news you wanted to tell us?"

Dermot took a sip of tea and then sat the cup down. "Given your history of playing detective and the potential connection to your farm, I wanted to share some information with you." Again, Dermot looked at Quinn.

Hattie looked up with raised eyebrows. "I'm not sure if I would describe what we do as 'Playing detective.' I was a detective, and Quinn, Fiona, and Margaret have gotten pretty good at crime solving, too."

"Oh, now, Missus, don't go getting yourself bothered. I meant nothing by that. I've come to respect all of you." Dermot spoke with sincerity.

Hattie looked somewhat appeased. "Go on then; tell us what it is you know."

Dermot pulled out his phone and rearranged himself in his chair. "First, I'll show you the pictures I have. Then I'll explain why I have them."

All four women leaned forward to look at Dermot's phone. The first photo was of a young woman standing in the Irish countryside. She looked to be in her early twenties. The picture was old, probably from the nineteen thirties. The woman stood beside a good-looking man about the same age. They smiled happily into the camera. The second picture was of the same young woman, but she was thin and gaunt in this photo. Her expression was one of abject misery.

Quinn studied the picture and gasped, "Is that our farm in the background, Dermot?"

"It is, Missus," said Dermot. "It appears some hooligans dug up this poor woman's grave. Her left arm and hand had been moved from where it would have laid across her chest. It looks like someone stole a ring she was wearing."

Dermot continued. "The woman's name is Hannah Byrne. The Historical Society just happened to have these pictures of her. Otherwise, I wouldn't have connected her with your farm. Do you have any idea what that connection might be?" Dermot looked at Quinn expectantly.

"I've no idea, Dermot, but I know someone who might. I'll visit my grandmother tomorrow and tell you what I find out."

CHAPTER 2

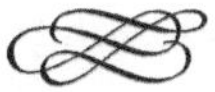

Quinn and her grandmother, Rose, seated themselves on the elegant linen chairs Rose kept at the back of her art gallery, which was in the town center of Skibbereen. There was a fine wooden coffee table in front of the chairs. It held delicate china cups and saucers patterned in little blue flowers with a matching teapot. Savory-looking biscuits sat on small blue plates that perfectly matched the blue in the flowers. Everything was impeccably arranged. Like most artists, Rose saw art in everything and was good at creating beauty, even when serving tea.

Rose's paintings covered the walls of the small gallery. Most were of the Irish countryside or the sea, with a few depicting interesting-looking vases filled with colorful flowers.

Handsome tables and chests held more miniature paintings. Well-placed, exquisite bronze lamps with pleated linen shades sat on several tables, giving the room a rich glow that played well with the art.

Rose was an elegant woman with thick white hair cut to just below her chin. She was small and thin and usually wore oversized, well-made shirts paired with designer jeans and black Doc-Martins. Attractive silver earrings swayed as she spoke, and she was seldom without the dark blue tanzanite stone that hung around her neck. Rose was in her early eighties, but only the hollow areas around her eyes bore testament to her age. In all other ways, she appeared much younger than her years. She still painted and ran the gallery by herself. Her mind was sharp and agile.

Quinn took a sip of tea and then realized Rose was staring at her. "What has you so troubled, Quinn?"

"Am I that transparent, or is the Knowing kicking in?" Quinn knew her grandmother well enough now to joke about her gift.

"A little of both, I'd say." Rose laughed and patted Quinn's hand. "Out with it, girl. What's troubling you?"

Quinn sighed and sat back in her chair. "Does the name Hannah Byrne mean anything to you?"

Rose thought for a moment. "You're talking about Pans. Her name was Hannah, but everyone called her Pansy or Pans. She died a few years before I was born. My family spoke of her from time to time. She was one reason I never wanted to see the inside of an Irish Home for Unwed Mothers. Pans died in one after they took her baby away from her. My mother said Pans only visited the farm once after they put her in that home. I think that was right after the baby was born. If I'm not mistaken, she died about six months later. It was always a chilling story to hear, and it gave me my first poor impression of the church. They never let most of the women out, you see. Once they stole their babies, they made them stay and work for the nuns. Some did that their whole life, others died, and a few lucky ones made it out."

Rose looked at Quinn thoughtfully. "How did you ever hear about Pans? I would have thought that story died out long ago."

"Dermot Brennan visited us yesterday. It seems someone has disturbed Hannah Byrne's grave. He said it could be hooligans, but the guards take grave robbing seriously, so they have opened an investigation."

"Robbing? You mean they took something from her grave?" Rose looked shocked.

"Yes, it seems so. They suspect that a ring was stolen. Pan's left arm and hand were roughly tampered with."

"They must have buried her with her engagement ring." Rose looked distressed and began rubbing the stone around her neck.

"You know something about her ring, Rose?"

Rose nodded. "Pans was engaged to be married, but the young man had no money. With Pan's urging, he decided to go to Tanzania, where they mined for tanzanite. He wanted to earn enough money so that he and Pans could marry and buy a little farm in the area. I believe his name was Killian, though I've forgotten his last name. Anyway, Killian brought back a large dark blue tanzanite stone and had an engagement ring made from it. Dark blue is the rarest color of tanzanite. Pans never took it off until they put her in that awful home. Her mother kept the ring then, knowing someone would surely steal it. She must have buried her with it, though."

"Tanzanite is not like a diamond, mind you, but certainly worth a fair amount, especially the dark blue ones. I'm surprised her parents didn't sell it. They were as poor as we were. I guess they felt it rightfully belonged with Pans. She certainly suffered enough in her short lifetime. I'm sure they weren't without guilt for what happened to her."

"As for Killian, he returned to Tanzania soon after he gave Pans her ring, and then she stopped hearing from him. Unfortunately, not long after he left, Pans realized she was pregnant. She was left to face the situation alone. Back then, your family disowned you if you became pregnant out of wedlock. The church gave them no choice."

"That's so awful. It makes me sad to think that her own family turned against her," said Quinn.

"Well, not her whole family. My mother had a kind heart. She was young and newly married herself and was friends with Pans. She had known her all her life. They had both grown up on farms in the area. Back then, people were close. They visited a lot. In the evenings, families would come together and tell stories by the fire or sing. My mother was very fond of Pans, so she took her in. Then, her parents and the church found out and forced Pans to leave. That's how she ended up in that horrible place."

"Wait," from Quinn, "Was Pans related to us?"

"Yes, of course, she was. She was my great aunt's daughter. She was my cousin on my father's side. I thought you already knew that since you said the Garda visited you."

"There was a picture of Pans in front of our farm. That's why Dermot thought it might have something to do with our family," replied Quinn.

"Do you have the picture? I know the one you're referring to. I haven't seen it in years." Rose looked at Quinn expectantly.

Quinn took her phone from her purse and showed Rose the picture.

"Look at that poor girl, so broken," exclaimed Rose. "My god, the church has so much to atone for."

"There's something else you should know about, Pans." Rose stared intently at Quinn for a moment and then continued. "She was another person in our family who had the Knowing. In her, it was very strong. When she was young, my mother said Pans would tell her family that she would have a child but never hold it and that she would not live to see her twenty-fifth year. Pans was the one who told Killian to go to Tanzania if he wanted to be rich and successful, even though she felt strongly that he would never marry her if he did." Rose sighed and looked away.

"There's one more thing I should tell you. Tanzanite enhances the Knowing. Pans must have seen her future quite clearly once Killian gave her that ring."

Quinn's eyes went to the stone around Rose's neck. "Is that why you wear that?"

"Yes. My stone is also a powerful one. Not all are. I've found wearing this stone helps greatly with my abilities and the emotions that come with it. It's not always a pleasant experience,... to know what's coming, I mean. Especially if you are helpless to change it. Pans lived her whole life knowing what was in store for her but, I'm sure, hoping it would not be that way." Rose sat back and closed her eyes momentarily, stroking the stone with her fingers.

Quinn left her grandmother's gallery, finding it difficult to process all Rose had told her. Mostly, she felt angry. Why was the church's treatment of Pans so cruel? Weren't they meant to help people in need?

When Quinn got home, she built a fire and poured herself a glass of wine. She listened to the crackling and popping of the newly lit fire for a moment and then sat down. Binx jumped into her lap and began to purr. Quinn stroked the kitten as Maggie turned in circles and lay down at her feet. Pike stared at Quinn intently as he made low, soothing little clucks from his perch. She smiled at the bird. Her creatures were such a comfort to her.

Soon, Fiona came in from the greenhouse. She poured herself a glass of wine and sat down. The friends sat companionably for a few minutes, and then Quinn related all that Rose had told her.

"How did the Church get away with that? It's just unbelievable. They made slaves of those poor girls." Fiona sighed and took a sip of wine, staring into the fire. "So, this means that Hannah Byrne and the Gillpatricks were related? And she had the Knowing, like Rose and Owen when he was alive?"

"Yes, I know. Can you believe that? I'm still processing the fact that the man we bought this farm from turned out to be my great uncle and that Rose is my grandmother, and then, of course, their gift of Knowing, and now this! A long-dead relative who also had the gift. And all that Rose said about the stones, the Tanzanite, I mean."

Fiona stared thoughtfully into the fire. "I wonder why someone would steal Pans's ring now, after all these years. And who would even know about it? Surely, there are people in the cemetery with more valuable items to steal. Why Pans?"

Quinn frowned. "I know. I've thought of that, too. It just makes little sense. This poor girl was a relative, though, and like Rose, found herself pregnant with no one to help her. I want to sort this out. What do you say, Fee? Are you up to another investigation?"

"Are you kidding? Of course I am! Let's meet with Hattie and Margaret in the morning." Fiona took a sip of wine and smiled. "I can't wait to get started."

CHAPTER 3

Quinn, Fiona, Hattie, and Margaret took their usual seats at the long pine kitchen table. This had become a ritual that they all loved and looked forward to. The leftover pastries from Margaret's B&B lay on a large platter in the center of the table. Everyone had their tea, and they were now, each, deciding which delicacy to choose.

Fiona reached for a piece of Irish Apple Cake. Quinn grabbed a raspberry scone, and Hattie settled on traditional Irish Soda bread.

Finally, the women were ready to talk about Pans. Quinn relayed everything she had found out from Rose.

Margaret was the first to speak. "Should we check with the church to see Pans's birth and death records? That's always a good place to start."

"Good idea," from Hattie. "We need to gather as much information as we can about her. And let's not forget Killian. We need to track down his last name and find out if he ever came back to Ireland to live or if he stayed in Tanzania. Also, where did they place the baby? We must start with those questions and work our way forward."

"Spoken like a true detective!" From Fiona. "And we should locate the home they put Pans in and try to get their records. Those would be useful."

"Good thinking!" From Hattie.

"I wonder how the ring plays into all of this? Somehow, I think it's the key to everything. I'm still shocked that Rose feels a tanzanite stone has power, but who am I to say it doesn't? Rose has abilities. I can't deny that. I wouldn't be alive without her gift," said Quinn.

After her friends left, Quinn walked out into the fields. She stood for a moment near the stream, watching as the water rushed over the smooth stones. Rose had, as a child, played by this very stream. She had collected stones. They had taught her the beauty of ordinary things. That idea had infused her whole life. Quinn caressed the stone in her pocket. It was one that Rose had found in this stream long ago. She had named it The Watcher Stone. Rose believed it had the power to protect the person who carried it. She had given it to Quinn to keep her from harm. Did Quinn believe in its power? If not, why did she always keep it with her? She had to admit; she did believe. But Quinn also felt that whatever our minds assigned power to automatically became powerful. So, which was true? And did it even matter? Quinn wasn't sure it did. She turned her mind back to Pans and her baby: so many questions and so few answers.

Quinn walked to the pigs' enclosure. She gently stroked Hilda's head. Hilda made pleasant little grunting noises as she leaned into Quinn's hand. Tam hurried over, wanting her share of the affection. Quinn obliged by rubbing behind her ears, knowing that was Tam's favorite spot. Then, she watched Newman strut across his enclosure. He was a beautiful cream-colored rooster with red markings, and he walked with so much confidence. Quinn chuckled to herself. She wished she could go through life with as much self-assurance as Newman.

Next, Quinn visited the miniature donkeys. She was happy they had settled in so nicely and had readily bonded with her and Fiona. Donkeys were affectionate animals. They would bay with joy at the sight of you and put their heads in the crook of your arm once they knew you. Quinn and Fiona were happy to have them as part of their family.

Once she had finished visiting the donkeys, Quinn began walking back towards the cottage. Suddenly, she felt strange. She blinked and shook her head, and continued walking. She had the odd sensation that something was taking her over. A foreboding seemed to snake its way through her body, a coldness. Then, Quinn heard a voice that was not her own. It kept repeating, bring back my ring, bring back my ring. Quinn felt frightened. What was happening to her? Next, she felt a jolt as though something had pushed her. The voice in her head started again, louder this time. Bring back my ring, bring back my ring. Quinn was terrified. She ran back to the house.

Once in the cottage, Quinn built a fire and poured herself a strong gin and tonic. She was still breathing heavily as she sat staring into the flames, gulping down the drink.

Fiona entered the room and looked at her friend. "Quinn, what's wrong? What on earth has a hold of you?"

Quinn rubbed her temples for a moment. "I don't know, Fee. Something happened when I was with the animals." She took another large sip of the gin and tonic. "I heard a voice in my head. I've never had an experience like that before. Like someone was talking to me in my head."

Fiona sat down opposite Quinn. "What did the voice say?"

Quinn thought for a long moment before replying. "The voice kept repeating, bring back my ring, bring back my ring.

It was like a megaphone in my head. I've never experienced anything like it. Maybe all this talk about Pans is affecting me. Jesus, Fiona, maybe this is all just too much for me!"

Fiona stared at her friend, then she spoke. "Have you ever considered that you might have inherited the Knowing?"

Quinn took another gulp of the gin and tonic, then slowly made eye contact. "Oh, Fee, I don't want it! Who would want that?"

Fiona put her arm around her friend. "Quinn, I understand how you feel, but think about how we ended up here. Remember our first time in Daily Kneads when the funeral procession walked by? You felt we belonged here. Maybe that was the Knowing? Our lives are so much richer now because of your epiphany. If you have that gift, it isn't a bad thing. I'm sure of that." Fiona smiled at her friend of so many years. "Please, don't worry, Quinn. Talk to Rose, but I'm certain, if it is a part of you, it's a good part."

CHAPTER 4

Quinn, again, found herself at her grandmother's gallery. This time, though, she was so shaken that Rose had closed the gallery and taken Quinn upstairs to her flat.

Quinn sat in the small living room as Rose made tea. She studied the room for a moment. Artwork covered the cream-colored walls as light streamed through the tall front windows. They were south-facing and overlooked the street. A small, cream-colored sofa with pillows in lively patterns sat against the wall opposite the windows. Two chairs in an appealing floral design completed the seating arrangement. Several antique tables held knick knacks portraying animals. Atop the table, nearest Quinn, sat a lovely bronze rabbit. An old-fashioned black-painted fireplace with a Victorian-style clock on its mantel and a framed photo of Rose and Owen added to the homey feel of the room. Quinn stared at the picture for a moment. It left no doubt as to the closeness of the siblings. Quinn wished she had known Owen better. Then she sat back in quiet contentment. The room was so pleasant. It enveloped her in the most comforting way. All the fear from the night before left her. She watched the light play across a painting with green fields bordered by stone walls. Wildflowers and ferns randomly poked their heads out between the stones.

Quinn sighed deeply just as Rose entered the room carrying a tray with tea and various biscuits. "Here we are, Quinn. This will make you feel better." Rose handed Quinn her tea. "We can stay here and chat for as long as you like. Honestly, it feels good to be of use to you." Rose smiled as she artfully arranged the flowered china teapot and matching plates on the table. "There now." Rose sat back, pleased with her work. Quinn thought again about how everything was art to Rose. She saw beauty in the simplest of things.

Quinn smiled. What an odd feeling it was to be cared for, nurtured even. Her mother had never done that. It added to the dreamlike quality life had taken on since hearing the voice. Quinn was completely relaxed now. For a moment, she felt like she was floating outside her body. Then, faintly, she heard Rose calling her.

"Quinn, are you alright?"

Quinn reached for Rose's hand. "I'm okay, Rose. I've just never felt like this before. Something has happened to me I don't quite understand. That's why I'm here. I need your help."

"I'll help you in any way I can. You know that, Quinn. What is it you need?"

Quinn ran a hand through her hair. "I'm not sure what I need. I realize that for my whole life, I've had,... this feeling. Only I never acknowledged it. I always pushed it away, but a peace settled over me as I spent time with the animals last night. I felt a kind of clarity, like my mind had expanded."

Quinn stared at Rose. "I think you call it the Knowing."

Rose smiled. "Oh, Quinn. You have finally realized; I'm so glad. From the moment we met, I knew I could sense it. It may not be easy to accept, but it is truly a gift. It isn't anything to be fearful of."

Quinn sighed and sat back in her chair, feeling more herself. "I think I need you to tell me how this works." She looked at Rose and chuckled. "And do I control it, or does it control me? Tell me as much as you can about this gift of ours, will you?"

Rose patted Quinn's hand. "First, would you mind telling me more about your experience?"

Quinn related everything that had happened to her the night before, including hearing a voice.

Rose looked thoughtful. "I see." Then she sat thinking for a moment. "Well, Quinn. Let me think about where to start as to my experiences. You already know I was having them as a child, and so was Owen. Maybe it made it easier for us that we both had it. At first, it was just a feeling, like something was off or not right, and it still can be that way. Usually, though, now, it's more vivid. Like the times you've been in danger. I knew where you were and that you needed help. That came through clearly. I think both of us having the Knowing added to the intensity of those experiences. That may be why you couldn't push your gift away this time. It was, obviously, Pans's voice you heard. Since she was like us, it's likely the strongest experience you've ever had. I could count on one hand the times I've heard a voice. They were undeniably my most powerful experiences."

Rose realized that Quinn had a concerned, somewhat disconnected look on her face. She reached over and touched her granddaughter's knee. "Are you alright? I'm sorry if I've overwhelmed you with too much information."

Quinn had been staring out the window, and now she turned her face back towards her grandmother. "She's here, Rose. I can feel her. I can feel her sadness. She wants her ring back. It's her link to Killian and her child. She won't rest in peace until she has it back."

Rose registered the blank expression on Quinn's face and realized that Pans had been speaking to her granddaughter. So Rose spoke directly to Pans. "Who has your ring, Pans? How can we help get it back?"

Quinn lifted her left hand and began twisting her finger as though she were wearing a ring. Then, she slowly pointed to the bronze rabbit on the table beside her. "Go to where the rabbit is," she said.

That evening, Quinn sat by the fire sipping a glass of wine. Only this night was different. She knew she, too, had the gift of Knowing. She no longer feared it. Now, she only felt resolve. She would do her best to give peace to this long-dead relative. She had had so little of that in life. And Quinn could, most definitely, relate to that.

CHAPTER 5

Fiona sat by the fire alongside her friend. Earlier in the evening, Quinn had related all that happened that afternoon in Rose's living room. Knowing Quinn how she did, Fiona knew something had always been different. Since they were children, Quinn had been so perceptive about other people's feelings. So, it did not surprise Fiona when Quinn became a psychologist. She couldn't deny that she was now worried about her friend, though. Quinn had put herself in danger again and again for others. Fiona feared this newly discovered ability would endanger her even more. She was glad that Hattie and Margaret would be there tomorrow morning. She felt she needed their insights into this. One thing she knew for sure was that she would protect her friend no matter what, and Quinn would do and had done the same for her.

Margaret pulled plates from the cabinets and gathered silverware and napkins as Hattie made the tea. Quinn and Fiona sat at their kitchen table, watching the other women work. Neither had slept well the night before. Their friends had looked at their tired, troubled faces and, without a word, set about their work. Finally, everything was ready. Margaret poured their tea and sat down. She and Hattie exchanged glances.

"Well, now so." Margaret patted her hair, took a sip of tea, and continued. "Tell us everything and leave nothing out." She looked first at Fiona and then at Quinn. "Come on now, out with it. What has made you two look like something out of a zombie movie?"

Quinn had to laugh. "You may not want to be friends with me anymore once I tell you, Margaret." Quinn cocked her head to the side, opened her eyes wide, and did her best impression of a zombie. In an altered voice, she said, "I hear dead people." Then she looked at Margaret for a reaction.

"Jesus god, woman, you're just makin' it worse! Stop yer jokin' and tell us."

"She's not joking, Margaret. She does hear dead people, or at least one dead person by the name of Pans. It seems Quinn here has inherited the Knowing and is only now realizing it."

Margaret and Hattie sat in stunned silence. Quinn was nearly falling out of her chair with laughter, as was Fiona. Finally, Quinn wiped her eyes and took a sip of tea. "God, that felt good. I've been much too serious the last few days." She smiled at Fiona, who gave her an understanding look.

Then Quinn set about explaining everything, starting two nights ago when she had been with the animals and heard Pans's voice and what Pans had said to her. She told them about her trip to Rose's art gallery yesterday, how she had felt Pans' presence again, and that Rose had spoken to Pans directly. Then she explained how she had felt a ring on her finger and that the experience had ended with her pointing to a bronze rabbit on a table next to her and saying, 'Follow the rabbit,' only it wasn't her that said it. When she had finished, she said, "Okay, that should get you up to speed. Now, you can have me carted off to the nearest asylum."

"You're not joking about this, then? This really happened to you, Quinn?" From Hattie, who now had a solemn expression on her face.

"It did, Hattie, and I'm trying to come to terms with it. I'm also trying to figure out how to do what Pans is asking of me. That ring could be anywhere now. I think Dermot is right that it was probably hooligans. They could have thrown it away after realizing it wasn't a diamond."

Just then, there was a knock at the front door. Quinn looked out to see Dermot standing on the stoop. "This is getting to be a habit with you, Dermot," joked Quinn as she opened the door and motioned for him to come in. "Are you here to visit us, lovely ladies, or is it the pastries that have you coming back?"

Dermot looked as though he could drop through the floor. His eyes fairly bulged. He straightened his jacket and bounced on his heels. "Now, Missus, that is completely ridiculous! I've come on police business, and that's the only reason I'm ever here. I don't care a thing about women or pastries." Dermot seemed to realize how that sounded and corrected himself. "What I mean is, I do like women, a' course, and a good pastry always goes down a treat, but that's not why I'm here at all."

Quinn grinned and patted Dermot's arm. "I'm only teasing you, Dermot. But do come in and sit with us while you explain why you are here. I'll have to repeat everything you tell me otherwise."

Dermot flinched a little at the pat but regained some of his composure. "Well, if you're sure that's what you want me to do, then I will, a' course." Dermot strolled into the kitchen and sniffed, looking around the room but making no eye contact with anyone.

Margaret smiled and then pulled the chair out next to hers. "Dermot Brennan, just the man we need! Sit down here and have some tea and a scone. You may have news for us, but we have news for ye as well." Margaret rose to fetch another plate, cup, and saucer. "Now, so, what is it you've come to tell us, Dermot?"

"I came to update Quinn on the latest developments regarding the grave robbery. As we now know, she's related to the deceased woman." Dermot looked ill at ease and fiddled with his jacket. "But I guess I can tell the rest of ye, too." He sipped his tea and gave Margaret a tentative look before continuing. "So, it turns out there has been a murder. A man, probably in his early fifties, was choked to death and dumped alongside a rarely used road about a mile from Ballyfrannen." Dermott took a large sip of tea and then continued. "The coroner figures he's been dead at least a week from the look of him. They identified him as a man drinking pretty heavily in Foley's pub about a week ago. He got to talking to some locals, and it seemed he was greatly interested in the very stone stolen from Pans's grave. The lads said he spent the whole evening telling everyone how much power that stone had, how his great-grandfather had found it in a mine in Tanzania, and how he had given it to a girl here in Ballyfrannen. According to him, that stone had changed everything for his great-grandfather. He said it had brought him luck and success. Only now, the mine wasn't producing any longer. He was about to lose the company his great-grandfather had founded. He thought the stone might be the key to everything and that the mine would start producing again if he got it back. This fella said he would pay handsomely for information about where to find the stone. He said he would pay even more to get it back. We reckon someone who knew about Pans and her ring overheard him and dug up her grave to steal the ring." Dermot sipped his tea and sighed. "Oh, I forgot to tell you his name, not that it will mean anything to ye. It was James Regan."

Just then, Quinn heard her phone ringing from the other room. "Hold on a minute while I get that, Dermot."

Quinn came back with a sober look on her face. "That was Rose. She has just remembered Killian's last name. She said it was Regan." Quinn took a deep breath, let it out, and looked at Dermot. "Not that there was really any doubt that the man you've been talking about was related to Killian."

Everyone sat in silence for a moment, absorbing this new information. Then, finally, it was Hattie who spoke. "Why kill the man, though? Why not just get the ring from the grave and take the reward he offered for the stone? We must be missing something. Why kill someone over his silly superstition about a not overly valuable stone?"

Quinn and Fiona exchanged glances, and then Quinn spoke. "For Pans, it wasn't a silly superstition. She believed the stone had power, that it increased the Knowing. Have you ever noticed the stone Rose wears around her neck? It's tanzanite, too. She believes it gives her more clarity with her abilities. Rose said that not all tanzanite is the same. She feels some stones are more powerful than others. She thinks that Pans's stone is extremely powerful."

Quinn rubbed her forehead, then raised her head to look at Hattie and Margaret. "Look, I'm not asking you to believe any of this. Even the part about me hearing Pans's voice. Only I know it to be true, and Pans has asked me to find her ring, so that's exactly what I will do."

Hattie reached for Quinn's hand. "Oh, Quinn, that came out wrong. I'm not saying I don't believe you. All of this is just so foreign to me. I'm used to dealing with facts. I've never dealt with anything supernatural before. But, of course, I believe you. I've known you long enough to trust what you say to be true. And I'll do all I can to help you."

"I believe you too, Quinn, in case there was any doubt," said Margaret.

Dermot was staring at Quinn. "Okay, missus, I think you'd better get me up to speed. What's this about hearing voices?"

CHAPTER 6

Quinn waited in Dermot's office. He had agreed to give her the names of the customers who had seen James Regan drinking in Foley's pub. She wanted Rose to examine the list in case any of the names sounded familiar. Quinn felt the person who had killed Killian's great-grandson must have some connection to Pans's family. A family friend, even, who might have passed the story down. After all these years, how else would anyone know about Pans or the ring?

As usual, Rose had the tea ready. Her china and freshly cut, fragrant flowers sat on the little coffee table in front of the linen chairs at the back of her gallery. When they were both comfortably seated, sipping their tea, Quinn pulled the list from her bag and handed it to Rose. Rose studied it for a long moment before speaking. "No name on this list stands out to me, Quinn. I remember some of these names, of course, but none has any actual connection to our family that I know of. Pans has been dead for so long, though. I don't think we would have any way of knowing who knew her story or who may have passed it down to others." Rose paused for a moment and looked at Quinn. "There is one thing about Pans's story I had forgotten, and it's not insignificant. About two years after Pans died, Killian came back. By then, he had made his fortune. Killian had loved Pans, but when the mine he'd bought was so successful, he had let it consume him. Then he came to his senses. He was heartbroken to learn what had happened to Pans. Even with Pans gone, he was determined to find his son and take him back to Tanzania. Killian hired the best solicitor in Dublin to help him find the boy. They found him in a children's home in Cork City."

"So, James Regan was probably a direct descendent of Pans. Still, why place so much importance on the stone Killian gave her? Did he really think that one stone could save his business?"

QUINN DROVE home feeling she was making no progress at all. Why had James Regan traveled so far to find a long-forgotten stone? Why was that stone so crucial to his family? So many questions and so few answers.

As Quinn drove into Ballyfrannen, she realized she hadn't eaten all day. Seeing a good parking spot, she quickly pulled in and headed towards Lizzie's for a bite. As she approached the cafe, she heard a familiar voice and then the sound of popping gum. She turned to greet Gracie, a twelve-year-old, sometimes patient and full-time friend. She had met Gracie through her grandmother, Sadie Fitzgerald, who owned the bookshop in Ballyfrannen. Since their first meeting, they had developed a shorthand that usually came with much lengthier friendships.

"Hey, Girlie, what ya up to?" From Quinn.

"Oh, nothing. Just running a few errands for my gran."

"Would your grandmother mind if you joined me for a sandwich at Lizzie's, do you think?"

Gracie thought for a moment. "I know for a fact that she would not, and a sandwich would go down a treat just now, but maybe I should run home to get some money from my gran first?"

"Nonsense. Sure, what harm would it do me to be buyin' ye a sandwich, so?" Quinn put on her best Irish accent, which caused Gracie to burst out laughing.

"Ahh, so, you'll never be foolin' anyone with that accent now. It's that bad; it is!" Gracie adopted a much thicker Irish accent than was normal for her in her effort to mock Quinn.

They were laughing as they walked through the open door at Lizzie's. Sitting down at a table near the window, they both studied the menu. Quinn decided on a Caesar Salad instead of a sandwich, and Gracie switched to a cupcake with loads of sprinkles.

"Why do ye have that worried look on your face, Quinn?" Asked the ever-observant Gracie. "Is there any way I can be of help?"

Quinn knew that Gracie was always willing to help others. She would never admit it, but Gracie reminded her of herself at that age. Gracie was wise beyond her years, and Quinn had been the same.

"Oh, I'm okay. I just came from a visit with my grandmother in Skibbereen. I always enjoy seeing her, but it is a bit of a drive."

Gracie dropped her head and looked grave. She seemed to have perfected Quinn's therapist face, which she now used on Quinn. "That's not why you look like that. There's something else. Am I not allowed to know? You know everything about me."

Quinn had to laugh at the face and the logic. "Good point, my girl. I do know an awful lot about you. I guess there's no harm in telling you. You've already heard about the murder of a man from Tanzania, I'm sure."

Gracie rolled her eyes. "Of course I have. I would have to live under a rock not to know about that since that's all anyone in town is talking about. What has that to do with you, though?".

Just then, their food came. Quinn waited for the waitress to leave before speaking. "I guess I'd better start at the beginning."

Gracie took a bite of the cupcake. Her serious expression contrasted with the effects of the sprinkles. Her lips were now a deep shade of blue. Quinn tried to ignore the blue lips as she related everything she knew about Pans, both past and present. She only omitted the parts about hearing Pans' voice and the Knowing. Quinn felt that was too much information for a twelve-year-old.

After taking another bite of the cupcake, Gracie sat wide-eyed momentarily as her lips turned an even deeper shade of blue. She then exclaimed, "That's the most fantastic story I've ever heard!"

"And one I'd ask you to keep to yourself." Quinn smiled at Gracie. Only the Garda and a few others know what I've told you.

Gracie gave Quinn a solemn look. "I promise, a' course." Gracie crossed her fingers behind her back as she spoke the words.

CHAPTER 7

Quinn studied her face in the bathroom mirror, noticing the dark circles under her eyes. What she needed was a night out, she decided. Colin had called several times to make dinner plans, but she had put him off. Now, that sounded wonderful. A mental break from everything would do her a world of good.

She and Fiona had spent all their time digging into the past, trying to discover as much about Pans and Killian as possible, but nothing new had presented itself. And, after all, wasn't this a job for the guards?

Quinn felt she wanted to tell Colin about her experience hearing Pans' voice and the fact she had the Knowing, like her grandmother and Owen and Pans. What would he think of her when he knew?

Quinn and Colin sat across from each other at a table in the restaurant section of Foley's Pub. Quinn loved the ambiance of the place. Old tile, checkered in deep orange and black, covered the floors. A small fireplace near their table glowed with wood and coals. Soft lighting and excellent food added to the relaxed atmosphere. Finally, Quinn felt the time was right to tell Colin about her experiences.

"Colin, there's something I think I should tell you." Quinn took a sip of wine before continuing. "I know we've talked about my grandmother and Owen's gift. We now know that Pans had it, too." Quinn paused again and played with the stem of her wineglass. "They were the only people in our family who appeared to have that ability." Colin sat patiently, watching her with a half smile on his face. "That is, until now. I, too, seem to have inherited this gift that Rose calls the Knowing. Recently, I had a rather unsettling experience." Quinn looked at Colin to gauge his reaction. To her surprise, he seemed quite amused.

Quinn couldn't help feeling annoyed. "May I ask why you're smiling like that? Do you find this funny?"

Now Colin was outright laughing. He reached for her hand and pulled it onto his lap. An act that Quinn found momentarily very distracting. She opened her mouth to protest his behavior, but the way he stroked her hand caused her to lose her train of thought entirely.

"Quinn, I know you're getting ready to tell me about hearing Pans's voice and what happened at your grandmother's, and I'm sure you're wondering what my reaction is. Only, you're forgetting that your best friend cannot keep a secret. I've known about all of that for days. I was wondering when you would get around to telling me." Colin continued to stroke her hand. "I don't give a damn if you come with extra gifts. Nothing will ever change how I feel about you. How I've felt about you since I first saw you." Colin pulled her hand closer.

Quinn tried to compose herself as she looked at Colin. "It's good to know I wasn't the only one feeling that way the day we met. I never believed in love at first sight until that day." Quinn immediately felt she had said too much.

Neither had ever used the word love before. She was mortified.

"Colin, I'm sorry. I don't know why I said that. I didn't mean…"

"Oh, but I so hope you did mean that." Colin had such a look of tenderness on his face. "I've wanted to tell you I love you for so long, and I do love you, Quinn. You've had my heart since that first day at the cottage."

Quinn took in his words. They filled her with so much joy. "And you don't think I'm a madwoman because of this so-called gift?"

Colin sat back in his chair and laughed. "Ahh, well, now. To be fair, I thought you were a madwoman long before I knew of this gift." Colin's eyes twinkled with affection.

The following day, when Quinn woke, she immediately thought of Colin and the wonderful evening they had spent together. She jumped out of bed and headed for the shower, knowing Fiona would want to hear about it. Not to mention Hattie and Margaret, who she was sure would come for tea this morning, knowing of her date with Colin the night before. Sure enough, as she dressed, she heard chatter from the kitchen.

All four women happily settled into their usual seats at the large pine table. Quinn waited to see who would first mention her date with Colin.

"Well, now so, are ye enjoying that pecan square, Quinn? I baked them special this morning, knowing they are your favorite." Margaret fussed with her hair, shoving it in different directions as she waited for Quinn to answer.

"Oh, stop buttering her up, Margaret. Do you think she'll give us more details if you ply her with food?" And then, looking at Quinn, Fiona added. "Is it working? We're dying to know how it went."

Quinn gave Fiona a slight punch in the arm.

"Hey, what was that for?" Fiona rubbed her arm in mock pain.

"You told Colin all about my experiences with the Knowing. So there I sat, like an idiot trying to get it out, and he already knew. Is nothing private?"

"It never has been before." Fiona took a large bite of strawberry scone with clotted cream and chewed contentedly. "I see no reason to start now. Besides, I knew you'd get worried about telling him and what his reaction would be, so I took care of it for you. You should thank me, not punch me."

"Actually, I was relieved he knew and had no problem with it. We honestly had a wonderful time last night. So, okay, thanks for getting that out of the way for me, I guess." Quinn smiled at her friend. "And, Margaret, these shortbread squares are as delicious as ever. So, you're free to ask me whatever you like."

"What did you have to eat?" From Fiona. Everyone laughed, and then the three women began bombarding Quinn with questions.

As they talked, Binx's head popped up occasionally from Fiona's lap as he waited expectantly for stray crumbs from her plate. Maggie and Wolfie slept peacefully under the table, and Pike perched on the kitchen sink faucet, ensuring nothing was happening outside that needed his attention.

Quinn chatted happily about the evening she had just spent with Colin, enjoying the company of her friends and again feeling grateful for her life in Ireland. Knowing how Colin felt made it all even more extraordinary. She stared out the window for a moment in a blissful fog. Then, suddenly, her mood changed. She felt terrible grief, and the voice again spoke to her. 'Bring my ring back to me, please, my ring.' Next, she heard sobbing and the words, 'Go to where the rabbit is.'

The next thing Quinn knew, she was standing in the living room. Fiona was standing next to her, calling her name. Quinn closed her eyes and then opened them several times, taking deep breaths as she did. "Why am I in the living room? Fee, what just happened?"

"I don't know, Quinn. What's the last thing you remember?"

"I was sitting with all of you in the kitchen, feeling great, and then I felt grief, only it wasn't my grief. Then the voice again. It said to bring the ring back. Then it said to go to where the rabbit is. What could that possibly mean? Fee, I don't like this Knowing thing. I'm not good at riddles and don't enjoy wandering around the house in some trance. How long have I been in here?"

Fiona tried to hide her worry. "It hasn't been that long. First, you got up from the table and walked in here. I followed you. Then, for a few minutes, you seemed unaware of where you were or that I was saying your name." Fiona put her hand on Quinn's arm. "Quinnie, do you remember anything from the last few minutes?"

Quinn felt she was not yet herself. "I don't know, Fee." She paused for a moment. "I saw a house, at least I think it was a house. It was large and old and nothing I'd ever seen before. That's all I can remember, just that I saw an image of a large, ancient house."

Quinn walked with Fiona back into the kitchen, where the other two women sipped their tea in subdued silence. Quinn sat back down but could not shake off what had just happened. "What's happening to me?"

Fiona, Hattie, and Margaret exchanged worried glances. They had no answers to that question.

CHAPTER 8

Quinn felt she needed to see Rose. How was she supposed to cope with what was happening to her? She was beginning to resent this long-dead relative who wouldn't leave her alone. Remembering the looks on her friends' faces the day before, Quinn felt embarrassed. Hopefully, Rose will have some answers. It was early, at least an hour before the gallery opened, but Quinn had called to tell Rose she was coming. She knocked lightly on the door, and Rose appeared almost immediately. She escorted Quinn to the back of the gallery, as was usual. Rose had laid tea on the little coffee table. Quinn noticed there were scones instead of biscuits on the silver serving platter and smiled. Rose motioned for Quinn to have a seat and then poured them tea.

"What is it, my girl? What has you so troubled?"

Quinn was glad she now had a grandmother. She felt comforted by her very existence. Sitting here in her grandmother's gallery, she felt safe. She took a sip of tea before speaking. "I had an experience yesterday. I guess what you would call a Knowing. I was chatting with my friends in the kitchen when a feeling took me over. The next thing I knew, I was standing in the living room. I had a vision of a large, ancient house. Pans' voice said, again, to find her ring and go to where the rabbit is." Quinn gave a little laugh and looked at Rose. "Is that cryptic enough for you?"

Rose studied her granddaughter. "Quinn, I'm sorry this is so hard on you. Pans wants her ring back desperately. Why, I don't know. Why she spoke to you instead of me? Again, I don't know. What I do know is that I will help you in any way I can." Rose gave Quinn a reassuring smile. "We'll get through this together. You're not alone."

Quinn rested her head on the back of the chair. She was feeling more herself now for the first time since Pans had spoken to her the day before. "Thank you, Rose. Right now, I need all the help I can get."

On the drive home, Quinn suddenly wanted to visit Loch Hyne. It was a beautiful lake just outside of Skibbereen. Quinn had always meant to visit the place but never had. Now, she turned her Volvo around and headed towards it. The lake was large, and the scenery was stunning, even for West Cork. Quinn got out of her car and walked towards the lake. As she strolled, she thought, again, of the Knowing and then of Pans. How sad her life had been. Maybe that was why she wanted her ring so badly. Was that all she had to cling to from her brief life? Quinn reached into her pocket for the riverstone she always carried. She rolled it over. It felt smooth and comforting in her hand.

Quinn took in the beauty of her surroundings. Was there a more wonderful place on earth than West Cork? She wasn't sure there was. Just then, she stumbled over a large stone near the water. When she recovered, she realized a young woman was approaching. Where had she come from, and what did she want? It's probably a tourist looking for directions. Quinn arranged her face into a smile.

"Excuse me, but are you Quinn Langston?"

Quinn reacted with surprise. "I am. May I ask who you are and how you know my name?" This girl had an odd accent, one that Quinn couldn't place.

The girl laughed nervously. "I'm so sorry. I didn't mean to startle you. I saw you in Skibbereen, so I followed you out here." She paused a moment and gave another small laugh.

"Wait, I'm not doing a very good job of explaining myself. Let me start over. My name is Charlotte Regan. My father was killed a little over a week ago here in West Cork. I've come to collect his body and take it back to Tanzania. One of the guards told me that you and your grandmother are my cousins, so I sought you out. I think I just wanted to feel connected to someone here. I drove to Skibbereen to visit your grandmother, but when I saw you come out and get in your car, I followed you. I'm sorry if I've frightened you or intruded. I must sound mad."

Quinn regained her composure. "Well, you startled me, but I'm fine now." Quinn felt she was being a little rude. "I'm so sorry for your loss. What a terrible tragedy for you and your family. I'm glad you introduced yourself to me, and I'm sure my grandmother would be happy to meet you, too. She knows much more about your direct ancestors than I do if that's the type of information you're looking for."

"That would certainly be interesting. I've always wondered about our roots here. We've all heard how my great-great-grandfather left Ireland to find his fortune and returned with a ring he had made from the first stone he had mined. He felt the stone had great significance. Of course, the ring was for a girl, Hannah Byrnes, or Pans, as they called her, but I guess you know all about that. My family has passed that story down through the generations. Once the mine stopped producing, my father got it into his head that it would turn everything around if he could find that first stone. I tried to tell him that was nonsense and that he was grasping at straws, but there was no dissuading him."

Quinn studied the girl. She looked about twenty-five and bore a striking resemblance to the picture she had seen of Pans—the same eyes, dark blonde hair, slim figure, and smile. A chill went up her spine.

"You look a great deal like your great, great grandmother. I have pictures of her on my phone if you'd like to see them?" Quinn pulled out her phone and showed the girl the two pictures.

Charlotte gave a small gasp. "You weren't exaggerating. I do look a lot like her." The girl continued to stare at the pictures. Finally, she frowned and said, "This second picture is so sad. Pans looks so broken."

Charlotte raised her head. Her eyes became vacant. Quinn knew, at once, what she was seeing, the same as Rose had done with her. This girl had the Knowing. Did she realize, or was she unaware, the same as Quinn had been for so many years? Was it something she had pushed away and given no notice to? But she was here with Quinn, and Quinn knew that being with someone like you only enhanced the gift.

"Charlotte, are you alright?" Quinn gently touched the girl's arm.

"The rabbit. We have to go to where the rabbit is." Charlotte still had a vacant look and seemed to be unaware of where she was. Then, finally, she looked directly at Quinn. "You're like me, aren't you? I've never met anyone like me before. I just thought there was something terribly wrong with me."

"There isn't anything wrong with you, Charlotte. I am like you, and so is my grandmother. And her brother, God rest his soul, was like us, too." Quinn smiled at Charlotte reassuringly, "And Pans also had the Knowing, as Rose and I call it."

"Perhaps we should go back and speak with Rose. She's had her gift since she was a child. I've only recently discovered mine, so I'm afraid I'm not much help to you."

"I would like that very much." Charlotte allowed Quinn to lead her back to her car.

"Are you sure you're okay to drive now? I know these experiences can leave you feeling not quite yourself." Quinn studied the girl's face as she spoke.

"I'm fine now. And I would very much like to speak with Rose. I have so many questions, questions I've had my whole life. Maybe here, with you and your grandmother, I can finally find some answers."

CHAPTER 9

Quinn drove home from Skibbereen, deep in thought. She and Charlotte had returned to the gallery, only to find Rose had gone out. Now she wondered, again, why Pans was sending her and Charlotte the same cryptic message, 'Go to where the rabbit is.' What did that mean? Charlotte had promised to come to the cottage tomorrow. Quinn thought it might be better for the three women to meet at the farm, where they would have more privacy. Rose was eager to meet Charlotte and, like Quinn, wondered exactly what her abilities were.

That night, Quinn and Fiona sat beside their ancient fireplace sipping wine. The wind howled softly as the flames danced, casting shadows around the room. Their golden tongues reached upward, giving the impression of constantly changing entities. What would tomorrow hold when all three women gathered in this room, each with their gift of Knowing? All manner of incredulities now seemed possible.

Quinn had a fitful night. Aberrant dreams plagued her sleep. Her bed felt like a coffin. She pushed to escape. A baby's muffled cry caused her to weep for what she had lost.

The words, 'Go to where the rabbit is,' ran through her mind repeatedly until finally, morning light filled her room, and she lifted herself from the bed. As she passed a mirror, she saw the reflection, not of herself, but of Pans. Quinn sat on the edge of her tub and put her head in her hands. She couldn't go on like this.

Finally, Quinn showered and dressed. She was feeling more herself now. She headed towards the kitchen to make tea. Rose and Charlotte would both be arriving shortly. She looked at the clock and then busied herself with the tea. Soon, she heard a knock.

Introductions had been brief and subdued. Fiona laid the tea on the coffee table and sat beside Rose on the sofa. Charlotte and Quinn sat in chairs by the fire. Already, there was a palpable feeling of dread in the room. Quinn looked at Rose questioningly, not sure how to proceed. Rose gave her granddaughter a nod and began to speak.

"I think it would be good if we talk about our experiences with what I call the Knowing." Rose directed her gaze towards Charlotte. "As Quinn knows, I've been having these experiences since I was a child. My brother, Owen, had them, too. It was always a part of our life, so it didn't seem strange. It's been harder for Quinn. She has just recently discovered her gift. Since Pans' ring was stolen from her grave, Quinn has had a series of quite powerful experiences." Rose paused momentarily to see if Charlotte would speak, but the girl sat staring at her hands as she listened.

Rose and Quinn exchanged glances. Then Rose continued speaking. "May I ask what your experience with the Knowing has been? Maybe you call it something else. My brother called it by a different name." Rose looked thoughtful for a moment. "You know, it's odd that Pans has not come to me. I wonder why she never sought me out?" Rose's hand went to the stone she wore around her neck, and she rubbed it thoughtfully.

Charlotte continued to stare at her hands for a few more moments. Then she looked at Rose, but her eyes looked vacant as she spoke. "I've been with you, Rose. I just hadn't made myself known."

Fiona and Quinn gasped, but Rose raised her hand to silence them. "Why was that, Pans? Why didn't you make yourself known to me?"

Charlotte's voice was little more than a whisper. "In you, the Knowing is very strong. You understand about stones; you know how powerful they can be. My stone is very powerful. I was afraid you would keep it from me."

"Why would I do that, Pans? Why would I keep your ring from you?"

Charlotte's voice was still soft, "Go to where the rabbit is, go to where the rabbit…." Charlotte's voice trailed off as her head snapped up. "Was that me talking just now?"

"Not you exactly, Charlotte. Pans was speaking through you." Rose spoke gently to the girl.

Charlotte sat thinking for a moment, then looked up. "She's afraid of you, Rose. Why is that?"

Rose sat rubbing her stone, and then she spoke. "I don't know why Pans would be afraid of me. But it obviously has to do with the ring." Again, she looked at Charlotte. "Did you see or experience anything while she spoke through you?"

Charlotte thought for a moment. "I saw a huge house. It was red brick with large, arched windows. It would have been lovely in its day, but I saw it as old and run down with overgrown pathways. It's long abandoned, from the look of it. It's not somewhere I would want to visit. It seemed a malevolent and sorrowful place."

Charlotte sighed deeply. "To answer your question about my experiences with this gift, I haven't had that many, really.

Just a...," she laughed, "As you say, knowledge about certain things. I've never had anyone speak through me before." Charlotte shook her head as though still slightly amazed by what had happened. "I've kept whatever this is to myself, mostly. I didn't want everyone thinking I was crackers." Charlotte gave a little laugh.

"I can definitely relate to that." Quinn chuckled and looked at Charlotte. The tension seemed to melt from the room. "I think we should be done with this for today." Quinn looked for confirmation from Rose, who nodded her head in agreement,

"Well, I don't know about the rest of you, but frankly, I'm ready for a drink!" Fiona jumped up and headed for the liquor cabinet. "Is anyone else joining me?"

Everyone nodded their heads. Soon, all four women were sipping a glass of wine, each thinking about what had happened.

Finally, it was Charlotte who spoke."You know, it's so strange, but I feel more myself than I have in a long time. Being here with the three of you is so comforting. It doesn't feel like we just met. I feel like I'm with friends, family even." Charlotte looked at the women a little sheepishly. "That must sound ridiculous. Yesterday, we were strangers."

"It doesn't sound ridiculous, Charlotte. It felt like home when Fiona and I first stepped into this cottage. Owen, Rose's brother, and my great-uncle recognized me as his family. He had been waiting for Fiona and me to come to Ireland and buy this cottage. He was saving it for his family. I'm glad you feel the way you do. You are family, too, after all. Do you have much family in Tanzania?"

"No, not really. I was an only child. My mother died when I was eight. I would love to say I was close to my father, but that wouldn't be true. He shipped me off to boarding school in England soon after my mother died, and I hardly saw him after that. Just the occasional holiday here and there. I saw him right before he left to come here. He told me of his plan to get the stone back that my great-great-grandfather had given to Pans. He believed it would make him rich again. I told him that was absurd and tried to talk him out of coming. We fought, actually, the last time I saw him." Charlotte sighed heavily. "Then I got the call from the Garda saying he was dead,... murdered. I couldn't believe it. I still can't believe it. Why would anyone kill my father over some long-forgotten stone, or was it even about that? The Garda haven't been able to give me much information yet."

"I'll put a call into Dermott. He's a local officer and someone I know and trust. Hopefully, he can give us more information," said Quinn.

CHAPTER 10

Dermot sat in Quinn's kitchen, sipping tea and nibbling on a biscuit. "No scones or pastries today, then?"

Quinn chuckled, "No, those come from Margaret. Unfortunately, Fiona and I are not nearly as skilled in the kitchen as she is."

Dermot looked a bit disheartened. "And this young lady here is the dead man's daughter. Do I have that right?"

"Yes, that's right, Dermot. We were wondering if you have made any progress with the case. Unfortunately, Charlotte has heard very little from the Garda. I know they brought the Cork forensic team and also their investigators in, but I thought they would at least keep you in the loop." From Quinn.

"You would think that, wouldn't ye? I've been trying to get information regarding the death of that man. The Cork lads don't seem to be giving out many details, though." Dermot took another bite of biscuit. "I'm sorry for your loss, miss... Charlotte, is it?"

"Yes, I'm Charlotte Regan. Is there anything at all you can

tell me regarding my father's death?" Charlotte looked at Dermot expectantly.

"Well, as I'm sure you know, the last time he was seen alive was in the pub. He was found about a week later on a little used country road. It appeared he had been strangled. Other than that, there were no clues as to who might have killed him or a motive for the crime. As I'm sure you've been told, he talked about a stone in the engagement ring of an ancestor and his desire to have it. He offered a reward to anyone who could bring him the ring. That's about all we know so far. I'm surprised the Cork officers haven't questioned you." Dermot directed his gaze at Charlotte.

"I spoke with them when I first arrived. I told them everything I knew, which wasn't much. I doubt I was of any help. Everything seems to lead back to the ring, though. Why did my great-great-grandfather think it was so special? I've never understood that. And why did my father think that? Was he grasping at straws because his business was failing, or was there more to it than that?" Charlotte looked at Dermot questioningly.

"I wish I had those answers for ye, Miss, I really do." Dermot had a discouraged look on his face. "All this talk about supernatural goings-on isn't helping. Most people look at that as superstitious nonsense and give it no credence. I fell into that category until Quinn told me about her experiences. I know her to be an honest and sane woman. That means I must consider what she says credible, even if it seems incredible to me." Dermot frowned and pulled at his jacket before making eye contact with Quinn.

Quinn smiled an acknowledgment of his trust in her. It had taken them both a long time to recognize the true worth of the other.

"No one at this table is giving up on finding the person or persons who murdered your father, Charlotte, or on finding out why Pans's ring is so important. Rose feels the same, and I'm going to bring in two of my friends who will also be a great help, I think." Quinn gave Charlotte a reassuring look.

Charlotte looked as if she might cry. "It's so strange to sit here with people I've only just met and feel so comforted, so at home, even. I'm not used to that. I've been on my own since my mother died. You can't imagine how much this means to me."

Quinn patted Charlotte's hand. "It might surprise you how much we understand how you feel, but that's a story for another day. Right now, let's try and figure out what it is about this stone that has cost your father his life and caused Pans to want it back so badly, even from the grave."

The next day, Quinn and Fiona gathered all the women together at Lizzie's. They quickly brought Hattie and Margaret up to speed. Rose was as determined as ever to help.

"Have you still had no contact at all with Pans, Rose? It is strange she has contacted Charlotte and me but not you. And what did Charlotte mean, do you suppose, when she said Pans is afraid of you?" Quinn looked at Rose questioningly.

"To answer your first question, still nothing at all from Pans. A reason for her to be afraid of me? Your guess is as good as mine. I can't figure out what that means." Rose dipped her spoon into the seafood chowder she had ordered. "Mmm, you were right, Fiona; this chowder is delicious."

Fiona smiled as she tucked into her bowl of seafood chowder, and then she said, "I think we should dig deeper into Pans's life. What do we know about her, really? Only what you were told by your mother, Rose. Mothers tend to protect us from a lot of things. So maybe there is more to the story than we know."

Hattie joined in. "Funny you should say that, Fiona. I've been thinking the same thing. We need to know more about

Pans. It won't be easy to find much information about someone who died in the 1930s, but we should gather all we can."

Margaret nodded her head in agreement. "I'm going to ask some of the older people in the area if they remember any stories about Pans and her family or about her and Killian."

CHAPTER 11

Quinn and Gracie sat in Quinn's office at the Mental Health Clinic. Gracie seemed to want to talk only about Pans or the murder rather than her week. Quinn couldn't really blame her.

Laughingly, she finally gave up. "Okay, ask me whatever you like. I'll tell you as much as I can."

Gracie twirled her hair and spun around once in her chair before speaking. "Do you think they are closer to finding who killed that man? Have you or your friends found anything on your own?" Gracie popped her gum as she waited for Quinn to speak.

Quinn sighed her frustration. "No one seems to know anything about his murder. The patrons at the pub the night he died aren't talking. Maybe they don't know anything. I'm sure the guards have spoken with everyone, and my friends and I have spoken with many of them, too. Nothing."

"What about poor Pans? Have you found her ring?" Gracie looked at Quinn expectantly.

"Nothing on that front either." Quinn considered Gracie

too young to hear about anything supernatural, so she excluded that part.

Gracie sat back, disappointed. Then she had an idea. "I know, you need to talk to someone really old who might know more about people who lived back then."

"I agree with you. One of my friends is pursuing that line of inquiry. Talking to some of the older people in town, I mean."

"Well, I know a really, really old lady. Her name is Annie McClery. She lives down the little lane around the corner from our shop. My gran visits her sometimes. I went with her once when I was little but never returned. Her house scared me. She collects dolls, and they're everywhere." Gracie sat back in her chair and sighed. "I wouldn't be scared now, of course, since I'm twelve."

Quinn suppressed a smile. "Visiting that woman sounds like a good idea, Gracie. I'll check with my friend to see if she has already spoken to her. If not, I'll go myself."

Gracie looked pleased. "You should run everything past me. I'm here to help."

Quinn tried not to look amused. "I'll remember to do that from now on."

Quinn made a quick call to Margaret regarding Mrs. Mc'Clery. After being told that Margaret hadn't spoken to her yet, Quinn decided to stop by on her way home from the clinic.

Now, she stood outside the door of a run-down stone cottage on a little lane near the center of town. The roof looked in need of repair. The windows were no longer well attached and had become crooked with age. A long dead geranium in a cracked pot sat on one of the windowsills. Paint peeled from the wooden front door. Nothing about the place looked inviting. Quinn sighed and knocked on the door.

A faint shuffling noise could be heard inside the house, and the door was pulled open. Quinn smiled at the elderly woman standing in front of her.

"I hope I'm not disturbing you, Mrs. McClery. My name is Quinn Langston. I was wondering if I could speak with you for a few moments regarding some local history of the area. I'm friends with Sadie Fitzgerald. Her granddaughter thought you might be able to give me some insight into what life was like here in the 1930s."

The woman stood staring at Quinn for a few moments. "What would ye be wantin' to know about that fer? Oh, no matter, come in, and I'll put the kettle on. I'm that grateful for the company, whatever the reason." The woman was quite stooped and walked with a cane. She pointed to a wooden rocker near the fireplace and said, "Sit yourself there. I'll be back in with the tea." With that, she disappeared from the room.

Quinn thought for a moment and then called to the woman. "Can I help with the tea?"

"I can manage fine."

Quinn walked to the rocker and sat down. A coal fire smoldered in the fireplace. Ancient, dirty lace curtains kept the room in semi-darkness. There were two rocking chairs by the fire and a battered-looking sofa against one wall. Several spindly tables, one with a pink lamp and flared shade, completed the furnishing of the small room. It was, in every way, unpleasant. The most unpleasant feature of all was the dolls. As Gracie had said, they were everywhere. Some lined the sofa, while others sat on its high back. Dolls covered every surface, even the shelves on both sides of the fireplace. Eyes stared blankly from round faces, giving Quinn the sensation of being watched.

She was relieved when the old woman returned from the kitchen. The tea sat on a decrepit wooden tea cart, which she leaned on as she wheeled it into the room. She handed Quinn her tea and made her own. Then, Annie McClery sat down heavily and looked at Quinn.

"Now, what's this ye want to know about the 1930s?"

Quinn told the woman about the recent murder and that a ring had been stolen from the grave of a woman who had died in the 1930s. Then, she explained how they related to each other.

The woman listened intently as Quinn spoke. When Quinn was finished, Annie sat back in her rocking chair and sighed.

"I think about Pans from time to time. Her life was a terrible tragedy."

Quinn had not mentioned Pans by name, so she was taken aback. "You knew her then? You knew Pans?"

" Of course I did. Everybody knew everybody back then. I was eleven when she died, but I remember her well enough." The old woman rocked and sipped her tea as she spoke.

Quinn had a thought. "Do you know anything about a rabbit? Does that have some meaning? I have a reason for asking."

The woman looked at Quinn out of the corner of her eyes as she rocked. "A rabbit is the connection to the Otherworld. It is a powerful symbol in Irish folklore, a pathway to the supernatural."

Quinn thought about that a moment. "Do you remember anything...different... or special about Pans?" Quinn wasn't sure how much information she should give this woman.

The old woman laughed. "You're talking about her powers. Yes, I knew about that. My family was good friends with hers. Secrets were hard to keep back then."

Quinn took a sip of tea and then tried not to make a face as she swallowed, realizing the milk had gone off. She sat the cup on the table next to her, moving a doll's dress a little to make room.

"What was Pans like?"

"Pans was kind as a girl. She was fun and silly, like most girls. She would talk to me sometimes. I liked her laugh." The old woman paused for a moment. "Then she got with that boy." Annie Mc'Clery frowned. "I didn't know anything about men then. I was only a child. I don't think Pans knew about men either, though,... the way they can destroy your life." Annie McClery stopped speaking; she rested her head on the back of her chair as though momentarily thinking of her own life. "That boy certainly destroyed Pans."

"Do you mean because she got pregnant?"

"I mean, when he found out about her powers, he used her and then left her. She was the one who told him about the mine in Tanzania. She told him he would become wealthy there. I think he brought her back that ring because he felt guilty. He never intended to marry her. I think she finally realized that. Only by then it was too late. Her fate was sealed. There was nothing she could do. I'm not surprised she wants revenge. Who could blame her."

"Revenge? I'm not sure I know what you mean."

Annie studied Quinn, "You know more than you're letting on. I may be ninety-six, but I've still got my wits. What is it you're not telling me?" Annie cocked her head and waited for Quinn to reply,

Quinn looked at the woman, wondering how much she should divulge. She suspected the woman was doing the same with her, as she had not answered the question about revenge.

"I'm a distant cousin of Pans's. My grandmother is Rose Gillpatrick. She has...gifts of her own. I seem to have inherited those, too." Quinn looked at Annie McClery to gauge her reaction.

Annie visibly warmed towards Quinn. "Well, why didn't ye say so in the first place? How is Rose, by the way? I haven't seen her in years."

Good god thought Quinn. Everybody really does know everybody else in Ballyfrannen. Then it struck her that was a comforting thought.

CHAPTER 12

Quinn woke up with a headache. Her visit with Annie McClery had been so odd. The idea of Pans seeking revenge had unsettled her, and she had had a fitful night.

Quinn opened her bedroom window and looked out towards the stream. She could hear the gentle gurgling of the water as it moved quickly over the rocks. Wildflowers planted by Fiona grew profusely in a riot of color near the water's edge. Quinn looked up into the trees as she heard the almost rhythmic cawing of nearby crows.

She took a deep breath and tried to settle her nerves. Her friends could be heard gathering in the kitchen, which was comforting. Again, Quinn felt gratitude for the life she now had. Finally, her headache was receding, and her mood had lifted.

After showering, Quinn joined her friends. They all sat enjoying the fresh cranberry scones left over from the morning's breakfast at Margaret's B&B. Quinn had already told them everything about her meeting yesterday with Annie McClery.

"I wish I'd been there!" Fiona popped the rest of her scone into her mouth before continuing. "She sounds fascinating. I would have loved to have seen her house, especially all those creepy dolls! What she said about Killian using Pans sure puts a different spin on things. And what do you suppose she meant about Pans wanting revenge? That's kind of a frightening thought, a dead person seeking revenge, like something out of a scary movie. Do you think Pans could actually do that? And who would she seek revenge from, since Killian is dead too?"

"All good questions, Fiona. I certainly have no answers. I need to talk to Rose again. She has the most knowledge about the Knowing and how it works."

"That sounds like a good idea, Quinn," said Hattie. "I have never had experience with anything supernatural. I think Rose is your best resource."

Margaret looked at Quinn, "This being Ireland, I've heard all sorts of stories about the supernatural. The Irish take that sort of thing very seriously." Then, Margaret looked at her friend with a troubled expression and added, "Just be careful, Quinn. There are forces in this world that we don't understand. But just because we don't understand them doesn't mean they aren't real….and sometimes dangerous."

"I'll be careful, Margret. I think I'll invite Charlotte to go with me to see Rose this afternoon. Maybe since she also has the Knowing, the three of us can find a way to figure this out."

Later that day, Quinn, Rose, and Charlotte sat in Rose's living room. Rose felt this was far too private to discuss in her gallery.

"I'm so glad you spoke with Annie. I hadn't even thought of her; in truth, I assumed she had died." Rose stirred her tea thoughtfully and then continued. "It makes me so sad to think that Killian used Pans. Men can, at times, treat women so horribly." Rose paused, and Quinn realized she was thinking about her own experiences.

Then, Rose continued. "The idea that Pans might want revenge is an interesting one. I've heard stories of people seeking revenge from beyond the grave. Like you, though, I don't understand who she would seek revenge from."

Suddenly, Quinn noticed that Charlotte's posture had changed. She was sitting very upright and was staring straight ahead. "Charlotte, are you alright?"

Charlotte turned towards Quinn, but it wasn't Charlotte who spoke. "Killian never loved me. He wanted to be rich and important. I knew how to give him that. I told him where to go to find it. Then, he betrayed me. He gave me the ring to soothe his conscience; only he didn't realize he was making me more powerful. The stone he gave me is potent. My family took it away when they sent me to that home. When I was dying, my mother came to visit me. I begged to have the ring back. I was buried with it on my finger. With the ring, even in death, I made Killian pay for what he had done to me. He knew no peace. His power and wealth gave him no happiness. I forced him to come back for our son. I wanted my son to have the life of wealth and privilege that was denied me. And then to have my grave defiled by my great-grandson. To have my ring stolen by my own flesh and blood. He hired men to do it for him. They knew my ring was buried with me. That rekindled my need for revenge. I became so angry. I am still angry. I want my ring." Charlotte's eyes narrowed to slits as she whispered, "Bring. Me. My. Ring."

Charlotte seemed to have been thrown back in her chair. She slumped for a moment and then regained her senses.

"My god, I heard everything, but that wasn't me talking." Charlotte looked at Quinn with eyes full of terror.

Rose said, "Now I understand why Pans never came to

me. I am as powerful as she is. She fears me. She knows I would have realized what she has become. She knows I would never help her get her ring back only to harm others with her power."

Charlotte looked at Rose. "Can you help me, Rose? I don't want to help Pans. I want to be free of her."

"Yes, I think I can help you. Is there anything you are holding back? Have you told us everything?"

Charlotte began to sob. "No, I haven't told you everything. I didn't come to Ballyfrannen after my father died. I traveled with him to Ireland. The night he died, I was there. Two men from the pub approached him and told him the story of Pans. They told him the ring was probably buried with her. My father didn't care that Killian had ruined her life. He only cared about himself. He wanted the ring because he thought it would do for him what Pans had done for Killian. He agreed to meet the men later that night. They left the pub and dug up Pans's grave."

Rose spoke in a kind voice. "What happened after those men stole the ring?"

"My father met them on a country road. He gave them the money, but they didn't give him Pans' ring. When he tried to take it, they killed him. I saw them do it; I was in the car. My father had said to hide when they arrived. They had no idea I was there. When they left, I drove back to town. I was going to the Garda Station, but I never made it there." Charlotte paused and took a ragged breath, wiping tears from her eyes. "A fog settled over me. It was like I didn't have free will anymore. Like I was being controlled by someone or something else. It's been that way ever since. I didn't remember being with my father that night until yesterday. I didn't keep it from you or the police intentionally."

Charlotte sobbed harder. "I don't understand any of this. What is happening to me?"

Charlotte tried to regain her composure. "I'm sorry I didn't tell you everything yesterday, as soon as I realized. This isn't the way I usually behave; it's just that I was so frightened. I'm still afraid."

Rose again spoke in a kind voice. "Charlotte, this wasn't you. It didn't come from you. What you did was because of Pans. She made you forget what happened. Don't you see that? You're not to blame. I think she knows where the ring is, too. I think that's what she's been trying to tell us."

Charlotte looked from Rose to Quinn. "Then you don't hate me? You don't think I'm evil? I was so happy to think that I had finally found my family. It was wonderful to feel like I was where I belong. I was so afraid to tell you what I'd done."

Quinn took Charlotte's hand. "It wasn't you, Charlotte. So why would we hate you? I know how powerful Pans is. I've experienced it myself."

"Charlotte, you have to figure out where the ring is. Pans won't stop until we find it." Rose spoke with certainty.

CHAPTER 13

Fiona looked at Quinn with a worried expression. "Quinnie, I hate that this is so hard on you. I wish this Pans would stay in her grave and leave you, Rose, and Charlotte alone."

Quinn looked up from the fire. She had had another fitful night. Her face was full of tension, and dark circles were visible under her eyes. "I never thought I would hear you say something like that." Quinn laughed. "Look how far we've come. Now we're dealing with dead people."

Fiona laughed despite herself. "I'm glad you still have your sense of humor, Quinn. I want this to end, and I know you do, too."

"I do feel like we're close to solving this. Charlotte's remembering more and more. We've turned all of her information over to the Garda. Oh, and I forgot to tell you, I talked to Dermot today, and he wants us to take Charlotte to Foleys tomorrow night to see if she recognizes anyone there. He's hoping she can identify the two men who killed her father."

"Well, at least we can take Margaret, Danial, and maybe even Colin with us so that it won't be all doom and gloom."

THE NEXT EVENING, Quinn and Fiona, along with Margaret, Daniel, and Colin, were seated in a booth on the pub side of Foleys. Charlotte wasn't far behind. They all ordered drinks and then attempted normal conversation.

Charlotte looked around the pub. "You know, this is the closest I've come to a night out since I've been here. It's ironic that I'm here to find my father's killers." Charlotte took a large drink of the Moscow Mule she had ordered.

"Careful, girl, those have quite a kick. You want to have your wits about you tonight." Margaret's voice was a bit scolding.

Charlotte smiled. "I'll be careful, Margaret. It feels good to be out with all of you, regardless of the circumstances."

Margaret's face softened. "I understand, lass. God knows you could use a night out with a few stiff drinks. I only want to ensure that if those lads are here tonight, you can identify them."

The booth was crowded, but Quinn was glad to have an excuse to sit so close to Colin. His presence gave her comfort the way it always did. She noticed Daniel and Fiona enjoying the closeness, too. Daniel visited the farm often now, and Fiona was always happy to see him. They wandered among the animals for hours, chatting about this and that. Daniel was even beginning to share Fiona's love for plants. Quinn smiled at Fiona in a way that telegraphed her thoughts to her friend of so many years. Fiona smiled back in acknowledgment.

Suddenly, Quinn heard a sharp gasp from Charlotte, sitting on her other side. "Charlotte, are you alright? Have you seen someone suspicious?"

"Oh, Quinn, I have! Those two men who just walked in. I'm sure that's them."

The men were in their late twenties or early thirties and rough-looking. Their clothes were dirty and stained. After sitting down at the bar, each ordered a shot of whiskey and a Guinness. They quickly downed the shots. Then, the men took long pulls from their pints of Guinness. Both scanned the room frequently as they spoke quietly to each other.

Quinn looked at the men and then back at Charlotte. "Are you positive, Charlotte?" When she didn't respond, Quinn looked at her more closely. Charlotte's vacant eyes and expressionless face told Quinn everything she needed to know. Quinn quickly called Dermot, who had stationed himself and a few men a short distance from the pub. Then anxiety set in. She had no idea what Pans was really capable of.

A moment passed, then Charlotte slid from the booth. Quinn called after her, but Charlotte didn't look back. 'Dear god, let Dermot get here fast,' thought Quinn. Everyone else at the table seemed frozen, unable to move. Quinn was feeling it, too. She tried to rise to follow Charlotte but was unable to. Instead, she watched as Charlotte approached the men. At first, they looked pleased, but as Charlotte leaned towards them and spoke in a low voice, their expressions changed to fear and then outright terror.

Quinn expected them to run, but they did not. Instead, they did nothing. Neither moved. Quinn realized that whatever she and her friends were experiencing, these men were experiencing it, too.

Suddenly, there was a loud clamoring at the door. Dermot and two other guards burst into the pub. Charlotte took a few steps back. She then raised her arm and pointed at the two men as the guards approached.

Dermot wasted no time. He and another guard handcuffed the two men. They offered no resistance as they were led out of the bar into different Garda vehicles. Dermot stayed behind. He spoke to Charlotte briefly and then walked to the booth where Quinn and her friends were seated. "Well, that's that, Missus! Charlotte gave us a positive ID on those two men." Then Dermot seemed to realize something was off. "Are you okay, Missus? You look strange;" then he looked around the table. "What's going on with all of you?"

Quinn could feel herself returning to normal. "We're okay, Dermot. To say anything more would only confuse you."

"I'll leave it at that for now, but soon, we're going to have a long conversation, Missus." Dermot gave Quinn a stern look. "Now, I'd better be gettin' to the Garda station and start questioning those men."

Quinn sat back in the booth and took a long breath. Colin reached for her hand. "Can you tell me what in the bloody hell just happened? I felt glued to this booth. I couldn't move a muscle."

Quinn tried to say something. Then, the absurdity of the situation hit her. She began to laugh. Colin's look of disbelief only served to make her laugh harder. She looked at Fee, who now snorted with laughter herself. Daniel and Colin were both looking at them like they had gone mad. Then, Margaret slammed her hand down on the table and let out a bellow of laughter. All three women looked at each other in disbelief, knowing this was totally inappropriate but unable to stop themselves. Finally, Quinn wiped at the corners of her eyes and said, "Oh, my god, Colin, the look on your face! I'm sorry; I know I shouldn't be laughing. Only, we've just been taken over by a dead woman. The ludicrousness of it just hit me."

Fiona let out another snort of laughter. This led to more

laughter from Quinn and Margaret. Finally, Fiona got control of herself. Quinn and Margaret followed suit.

The two men continued staring at them like they had lost their minds.

CHAPTER 14

The day after the arrests, the women sat in the kitchen, sipping tea and discussing the events of the previous evening. Charlotte had asked to join them. She wanted to tell them what she could about her experience at the pub.

Margaret set a cup of tea and a pecan square on the table. "Now then, pet, out with it. What in the name of heaven happened to ye last night, and for that matter to us?"

Charlotte took a sip of tea and sighed heavily. "I'll tell you as much as I remember. When I'm having one of those experiences, I feel like an observer in my own body. I have an idea of what is occurring but no way to control it. It's not a pleasant sensation. I can tell you that." Charlotte looked at Quinn. "I know you have had similar experiences."

"Yes, and you're right. They aren't pleasant. You feel completely helpless."

Charlotte nodded her head in agreement. "That's a good way of describing it. One minute, I was sitting in the booth next to you, and then I felt Pans. It was like a cold sensation, starting in my spine and then snaking through my body. I remember walking over to those two men. I felt terrified. I leaned close to their faces, even though I didn't want to, and whispered, 'I know what you did.' I saw the look of fear in their eyes. Then I said, 'Never go near my ring again, or you will be in your graves the same as I am in mine.' That must have truly scared them. Maybe they saw Pans in me. I don't know, but they told me where the ring is, and I remember Pans telling me to bring it to her."

Charlotte stared at the table for a moment. "If I don't take her the ring, she'll never stop. I'll never be free of her." She looked at Quinn. "I'm so scared. I don't want to live like this for the rest of my life."

Quinn gave Charlotte an understanding look. Just then, the doorbell rang. Fiona opened the door to find Dermot standing on the stoop. She pointed towards the kitchen.

"Everyone is in there."

Without a word, Dermot headed towards the kitchen. Fiona followed him in. Once they were all seated, Dermot began to speak. "Those two fellas confessed to everything. They dug up Hannah Byrnes's grave and stole the ring after they talked to Charlotte's father at the pub."

"One of them remembered his grandmother telling the story of Pans and her ring and the terrible things that happened to her."

"They decided to get the ring and then meet Charlotte's father. They wanted a place where there was no one around. The idea was to take the money and keep the ring for themselves only; Mr. Regan put up a fight. The bigger man punched him. When Regan still tried to get the ring and his money, he choked him. Then, the two of them hid the ring somewhere. They were frightened they would be implicated in his death if they held on to it."

Dermot sat back in his chair and sipped his tea before continuing. "Neither would tell us where they've hidden it, though. We'll keep trying, but they seem fearful whenever we talk about the ring. Any reason for that that you can think of?" Dermot looked first at Quinn and then at Charlotte.

Quinn spoke first. "We don't know any more about it than you do, Dermot." When Dermot looked away, she glanced at Charlotte and shook her head. Charlotte understood.

"No, we're completely in the dark about that." Charlotte sighed and clasped her hands together on the table.

Dermot seemed less than convinced. "Listen, ladies, if there's anything you're not tellin' me, now is the time." Dermot pulled at his jacket for a moment and sniffed. "All this supernatural talk has me spooked. No pun intended." Dermot cleared his throat before continuing. "I just want you to let us handle this from now on. Don't go gettin' yourself into anything without havin' me along to protect ye." Dermot looked at Quinn accusingly.

Quinn laid her hand on his arm. "Dermot, we appreciate your concern. No one knows more than me what an asset you are in times of danger. If we need help, you'll be the first person we call."

Dermot seemed more satisfied. "Okay, then, Missus. I'll hold you to that. Now I've got to be gettin' back to the Garda station. Those men need to be processed and booked. I'll keep trying to get more information out of them regarding the ring, too." Again, he looked from Quinn to Charlotte.

"We appreciate that so much, Dermot." With that, Quinn led him out and closed the door, more determined than ever to find the ring.

CHAPTER 15

Quinn felt she should bring Rose up to date on all that had happened. So she headed back to Skibbereen the following day.

Rose sat in her gallery, waiting for Quinn to arrive. She was more concerned about her granddaughter's safety than she cared to admit. For so many years, it had just been her and Owen. When she moved back to Ireland, she had let Keavy, and consequently, Keavy's daughter, recede to the back of her mind. Almost as if they didn't exist. She felt ashamed of that now. Why had she not been a part of her granddaughter's life in America? Now, she loved Quinn so much. Something that could never truly be said about her own daughter: try as she might, Rose could never forget how Keavy came to be, and even though that wasn't Keavy's fault, she had paid the price for it.

For a moment, Rose relived her time working for the parish priest. Her innocence had been stolen at such a young age. The dreadful horror of being raped, not once, but many times over the months she had worked at the rectory as a young girl was a memory that would never leave her. Then she had fallen pregnant, and the priest had sent her to America, to another priest just like him. Only then had she recognized him for what he was. His eyes had the same look in them as the other priest's. She understood that she was not safe, and she had run away. She was alone in a country she didn't know. If not for the kindness of others, she would never have survived. There were good people in the world, and they had helped her. She thanked God for that.

Rose laid her head back in sorrow for everything she would change if she could. Life didn't allow for that, though. She had to move forward, but she was determined that no one and nothing would harm her granddaughter as long as she was alive to protect her.

Quinn walked into the art gallery with a worried look on her face. Rose realized that Quinn had no idea what a lovely woman she was. She had dark hair and eyes like her mother, but she was prettier than Keavy. Or maybe Keavy would have been prettier if she had not been so troubled. Quinn had a good figure, not unlike herself, and Rose liked to think she had her smile. She felt pride in how her granddaughter carried herself through life, even more so since her life had not been easy.

Quinn sat down in the chair next to Rose and poured herself a cup of tea. Rose smiled but said nothing.

Quinn studied her grandmother for a moment. "You looked deep in thought when I came in. Anything you'd like to share?"

"No, just stray thoughts. That happens when you're older."

Quinn smiled at her grandmother and then spoke. "They have arrested the two men who killed Charlotte's father?"

"I'm so glad! How did they find them?"

"Well, that is a fascinating story, Rose. Last night, a group of us went to Foley's, hoping Charlotte would recognize the men she saw kill her father." Quinn stopped and stirred her tea. "Pans made an appearance of sorts. She took Charlotte over and approached the two men. They were terrified of her. Dermot arrested them last night, and they both confessed to the murder, but neither is telling where the ring is. Dermot says they seemed afraid to even talk about it. I think when Pans had possession of Charlotte, she warned them off of telling anyone but Charlotte."

Rose thought for a moment. "You're probably right, Quinn. She would want Charlotte to bring her the ring. Someone she knows she can control. Do you know where the ring is now?"

"Yes, Charlotte knows where it is and how to get there."

"Well, then, what are we waiting for? I think you, Charlotte and I need to find the ring. We are the ones with the Knowing, so it only makes sense that the three of us go alone. We don't want to scare Pans off. I think it's time she and I have a little chat."

"Do you mean right now?" Quinn felt terror pass through her at the thought of Rose confronting Pans.

"No, not right now, but tonight. Pans is much more likely to show herself at night."

"Oh great! That sounds even better." Quinn felt her stomach knot at the thought of the three of them confronting Pans.

CHAPTER 16

That evening, all three women sat at the cottage before the fire. Fiona had spent the last hour trying to talk them out of going alone. "At least take me with you. What if something happens? You have no idea what Pans is capable of. I think Dermot and I should both be going with you!"

Quinn gave her friend a fond smile. "I would feel the same if you were going instead of me, Fee. I think Rose is right, though. It has to be the three of us confronting Pans. This has to end."

Once dark, the three women set out in Quinn's Volvo. It hadn't escaped Quinn's attention that Pike had taken flight when they pulled out of the driveway. She could see him following closely behind the car. The thought of Pike being with her gave Quinn comfort.

"You're sure you know where the ring is, Charlotte?" Quinn waited for Charlotte to answer.

"Go down this road for two more miles and then turn left at O'Brian's farm."

Quinn looked at Charlotte questioningly, then Rose

spoke. "I know where she means. No one has lived in that house for years, but when I was a girl, it used to be owned by a family named O'Brian." Rose laid her hand on Quinn's arm before continuing. "Quinn, it's not Charlotte you are speaking to anymore." Rose then shot Quinn a cautioning glance.

Quinn's heart began to pound uncomfortably as she drove on.

Charlotte,...or Pans, continued to tell them where to go. Finally, they were on a little used road about ten miles from Ballyfrannen.

"Oh, my God, I know where she's going. There's an asylum at the end of this road. It hasn't been used in fifty years at least. It would be a perfect place to hide something you didn't want anyone to find." Rose sounded alarmed.

As they continued, the road got bumpier. Finally, a large brick building came into view. Quinn stopped the car at the edge of the property. The grounds were completely overgrown. There would be no easy path to the structure. The three women slowly picked their way through the brush, finally reaching the front of the building. A long set of stairs with a dilapidated railing led to a covered porch and the large front door. Quinn and Rose exchanged glances as they followed Charlotte up the steps. Quinn remembered seeing this same building the night Pans had taken her over. The thought only made her more fearful of what lay ahead.

Once at the door, Quinn saw a large brass knocker, green and crusty with age and shaped like an Irish hare. She thought of the words Pans had spoken through her at her grandmother's. 'Go to where the Rabbit is.' Then, she thought about how Annie McClery had told her that a hare was the connection to the Otherworld and the supernatural.

Quinn and Charlotte pushed hard on the door. It slowly gave way. Once inside, they realized they were standing in a massive foyer with a stone fireplace and a broad stairway. Moonlight streamed in through a large window with a broken pane. The smell of decay and rot filled their nostrils.

Quinn could feel the misery of the people who had occupied this place. She turned to Rose. "What kind of asylum was this?"

"It was a dumping ground for the insane, the weak-minded, the elderly, anyone who wasn't wanted. As I'm sure you realize, the people who ended up here were treated cruelly. Some were chained to their beds, others locked in rooms no bigger than closets. At times, they were starved and beaten. Most only survived a few years. In the back, there's a cemetery with hundreds of unmarked graves. There was a scandal years ago about this place. That's why they finally had to close it down. I've never understood the kind of cruelty that went on here."

Charlotte whirled around and snarled at Quinn and Rose, "Stop talking and find my ring."

Rose walked slowly towards Charlotte. She clasped the stone around her neck before speaking. "Pans, you think you are in control, but you don't control me."

Quinn could barely make out Charlotte's face in the moonlight; only it no longer looked like Charlotte's face. Instead, she saw Pans' face staring back at Rose, contorted with rage and hatred. "You think you're stronger than me?"

Rose only smiled. "I think you think that, Pans. Isn't that why you used Quinn and then Charlotte but never me?"

Quinn saw the fear that crossed Charlotte's face briefly before she, again, looked enraged. "I want my ring! I know where it is. This girl will bring it to me, and we will see who is stronger. Once I have my ring, I can possess her forever."

Charlotte ran up the stairs. Quinn and Rose quickly followed. Once on the second floor, Charlotte headed for a door at the end of the hallway. It was a large room. It appeared to have been a day room for the people forced to live there. There were high windows along one side. Rusty metal chairs and a few broken wooden tables were strewn across the floor, along with old papers and other disparate, decaying objects. The room smelled strongly of mold and other unpleasant odors.

Charlotte searched frantically through the clutter. She paid no mind to the stench or the filth. Then she came to an old cupboard. She opened it and threw objects onto the floor until she found a small box. Grabbing the box with a gleeful laugh, she ran from the room back towards the staircase. Rose quickly followed. She swiftly grabbed the box from her fingers and handed it to Quinn.

"Don't let her have the ring no matter what happens to me." Rose momentarily locked eyes with her granddaughter; Quinn hesitated and then gave a quick nod, fully understanding the meaning of her grandmother's words. Finally, Rose turned back towards Charlotte and faced Pans directly.

"You must go through me to get the ring, Pans. Do you think you're powerful enough? You know I can't let you have it, and you know why. You want to use its power to hurt others; I can't let you do that."

"You were a good person once, Pans. I know you were treated cruelly in life, and I'm sorry. But I can't let you continue to harm people. I have to take your power. It shouldn't have followed you to the grave. It wouldn't have if you did not have such a powerful stone. I will stop you now, Pans, before you ruin more lives. You made Killian pay for what he did to you, but now you're punishing an innocent girl."

Pans only laughed. "You think you can stop me? What if I kill this girl? Then how will you feel? Give me the ring, or I will do it." Charlotte stepped closer to the railing. The stone floor below was twenty feet away. A fall would surely kill her.

"That girl is your great-great-granddaughter, Pans." Rose took a step towards Charlotte.

"Don't come any nearer; I will send her to her death."

Rose looked at Quinn and reached out her hand. "She is even more powerful than I imagined." There was a desperate tone to Rose's voice. "Give me your hand, granddaughter, and hold tight to your stone. I can't fight her alone."

Then Rose looked hard at Charlotte. "Charlotte, I know you can hear me. Use the Knowing! Use your power! Fight her with all that is in you."

Pans took another step closer to the railing. Quinn and Rose gripped each other's hands and their stones. Pike flew in through an open window. He perched on the railing in front of Charlotte, extending his wings and lowering his head before giving a loud caw. Quinn was beginning to feel stronger, more powerful. Something surged through her. She could feel Rose's power, too. They acted as one. Each gaining strength from the other. She gripped the stone around her neck with all her might.

Suddenly, Charlotte collapsed onto the floor. Quinn knelt beside her. Pans looked up, and Quinn saw the rage drain from her face. Then she whispered. "You have won. I won't fight you anymore. Send me to my grave and keep my power. I don't want to harm my granddaughter. I don't want to harm any of you." She reached for Quinn's hand.

Pans lay on the floor sobbing momentarily as she held Quinn's hand. Then she was quiet.

"I want to be at peace now." Pans looked at Quinn one last time. Then, she was gone.

CHAPTER 17

Quinn pulled Charlotte from the floor. Then, she put Charlotte's arm around her neck and helped her down the stairs. Pike now perched near the front door, watchful and alert.

Once in the car, the women felt more themselves. Pike flew alongside, still keeping guard. It was Rose who spoke first.

"Drive to the church, Quinn—the one near our farm. We have to place the ring in Holy Water. Pans used the ring for evil. This is the only way to cleanse it."

Quinn did as she was told. As the little church and the rectory, where she and Rose had each known trauma, came into view, Quinn felt her heart thump in her chest. She remembered the Brazilian drug dealer who had pretended to be a priest. He had almost killed her when she found out. She thought of Rose and all she had endured in that same small rectory room.

She tried to put those thoughts out of her mind as she entered the churchyard. The women piled out of the car and headed towards the small church. It was unlocked. Quinn pulled at the door and walked in, followed by Rose and Charlotte. The marble font that held the Holy Water stood near the back of the church. Rose dipped her fingers in it and crossed herself. Quinn and Charlotte followed suit. Then, Quinn pulled the little box out of her pocket and handed it to Rose. Rose gently placed the ring in the font. Then she knelt to pray. Quinn and Charlotte stood watching.

Rose crossed herself again and stood up. She removed the ring from the Holy Water and walked towards Charlotte. "Hold out your hand, my dear."

Charlotte did as she was told. Rose slipped the ring onto her finger. Its brilliance sparkled in the moonlight.

"What does this mean, Rose? Why are you giving me the ring?" Asked Charlotte.

"Because now its power is free from the evil Pans gave it. You can wear the ring, and it will enhance your Knowing. Pans will never bother you again; she is truly at peace. This is what she wanted."

Charlotte stared at the ring for a long moment. Then, she and Quinn silently vowed to use their gifts to help others. Pike entered the church and perched on Quinn's shoulder. Quinn sighed deeply. She had no idea what the future held, but she now realized why she had come to Ireland. She had come home to her people and her creatures.

CHAPTER 18

Rose and Charlotte stayed with Quinn and Fiona at their cottage for several days. The closeness that had entwined them at the church was still present, and they felt the need to be together.

It had turned into an enjoyable time for all the women. A celebration that something terrible was finally over.

Hattie, Margaret, Quinn, Fiona, and Charlotte gathered in the kitchen for hours daily. Even Maggie and Wolfie seemed to realize it was a special time. Binx, the kitten, was also in good spirits. He loved to sit on Fiona's lap and eat the crumbs that either fell or were given to him by Fiona or the others.

The women ate more than the usual amount of pastries due to Margaret holding a firm belief that food solved most miseries. Quinn, Rose, and Charlotte each gave versions of what had transpired at the asylum. Charlotte's telling was the most frightening, especially about her being forced toward the railing and feeling Pans would push her over the edge.

Fiona, Margaret, and Hattie had all gasped with fright at what they heard. More than once, during the various tellings,

Margaret had slammed her hand down onto the pine table so hard and exclaimed Jesus God so loudly it had caused Maggie, Wolfie, and even little Binx to quickly exit the room.

Now, everything was slowly returning to normal. Even Pike seemed to be settling down after spending days at Quinn's side, never letting her out of his sight.

Fiona had also been affected. Her eyes would suddenly fill with tears at unexpected moments. At those times, Quinn would hug her friend, which usually led to more tears. It was good to be loved, and they all felt grateful to be able to spend this time together.

Now, they gathered once again around the big pine table. On this particular day, Quinn had asked Sadie if Gracie could join them. Dermot had offered to bring her. The pair now sat with the women staring at yet another platter of baked goods from Margaret's kitchen. Gracie's eyes were like saucers as she examined the unbelievably large pile of mouth-watering delicacies.

"Do you mind me asking how many I can eat?" Gracie used her most polite voice.

Margaret laughed good-naturedly. "Eat all you want, girl, only don't make yourself sick, or your gran won't speak to me for a week."

Gracie smiled with delight and reached for a pecan square. "You are a heavenly cook, Ms. O'Callahan."

"Just call me Margaret, lass." Margaret gave Gracie a warm smile.

Quinn studied Margaret for a moment. Then, "Margaret, are you wearing make-up? And may I say, your hair is looking particularly lovely today?"

Margaret looked more than a little flustered. "Oh, go on with ye. I just threw on a little powder, that is all. My hair isn't that much different, either. I had it cut and styled yesterday since you're being so nosy."

Fiona, too, gave Margaret a look over and then caught Quinn's eye. She proceeded to raise her eyebrows up and down a few times before chiming in. "If I didn't know better, Margaret, I'd say you have found yourself a fella."

Margaret quickly glanced down the table to where Dermot was sitting. He was happily oblivious to everything but the strawberry scone he was eating.

"That is the most ridiculous thing I have ever heard in my life. Can't a body fix themselves up a little without being questioned to death?" Margaret glared at Fiona.

Quinn and Fiona, along with Hattie, exchanged surprised glances. Quinn had told Margaret the day before that Dermot would bring Gracie to join them. Did Margaret secretly harbor feelings for Dermot, she wondered?

Still utterly oblivious to the conversation, Dermot smiled down the table at Margaret. "These sure are delicious scones, Margaret. Whoever gets you for a wife will be one lucky man."

Margaret's cheeks turned bright red, and she patted at her hair even though there wasn't a hair out of place. She opened her mouth to speak and then closed it again.

Gracie, who had caught on that something was afoot, turned her head from Dermot to Margaret and then back again as though watching a tennis match. Then, when Margaret still didn't answer, Gracie tapped her politely on the arm, "Guard Brennan is talking to you, Margaret."

This only served to confound Margaret more. She, again, patted her hair and continued to glare at Fiona. Fiona reacted by drawing a heart in the air and then pretending to shoot an arrow through it at Margaret. At this, Margaret made what she perceived as her angriest face and then said a series of swear words under her breath while shaking her fist menacingly at Fiona. Fiona was now rocking back and forth with silent laughter.

Gracie sat, taking it all in. Dermot continued happily eating his strawberry scone, still utterly oblivious to everything going on around him.

Quinn and Hattie sat watching the two women. Finally, Quinn sighed and shook her head. Then, she spoke to Dermot. "She does make the best scones, doesn't she, Dermot? You'll have to visit us more often. We get together several mornings a week."

"That would be great, Missus; I would love to visit with you lovely ladies from time to time." Dermot reached for yet another scone as he again smiled at Margaret, still having no clue that anything had transpired.

Then, the conversation turned to more serious topics.

Dermot reported that the two men who had killed Charlotte's father had been arraigned and would stand trial for his murder.

After Fiona had taken Gracie out to see the animals, Quinn, Charlotte, and Rose gave him a brief synopsis of the events that had transpired with Pans and her ring. It ended with Charlotte holding out her hand to show Dermot the ring that had given Pans so much power.

Dermot eyed the ring for a moment. Then, with a perplexed expression, he spoke to Charlotte. "And you're actually going to wear that thing after it was buried with a dead woman and all?"

"I am," Charlotte said proudly. "This ring's power will never again be used for evil," Charlotte spoke with pride as she looked down at the ring.

"Well, I like rings with no powers at all myself. I couldn't close my eyes at night with a ring like that on my finger." Dermot sniffed and pulled at his jacket, looking nervous.

"Look, I believe what you ladies are telling me, only it's a lot to swallow if you know what I mean. If it were anyone else tellin' me this, I'd tell them to stop pulling my leg."

Quinn gave Dermot a sympathetic smile. "I do understand how hard this must be to believe, Dermot. But it is true, every last bit of it."

Everyone fell silent for a moment.

Then Charlotte looked around the table. "You can't imagine how much this time with all of you has meant to me. I'm sure I've overstayed my welcome, though. I should look into getting a plane ticket for the trip home."

"Home?" Margaret looked up, astonished. "Girl, don't ye realize yet that ye are already home, here, at this table, in Ireland with us?"

"She's right, Charlotte. You belong here." Fiona, who had just rejoined them, spoke with sincerity.

Hattie joined in, "I agree with Margaret and Fiona; your home is here, with us. You could stay with me at my cottage until you find your own home. Wolfie and I would love the company."

Charlotte turned her gaze to Quinn and Rose. Quinn smiled and grabbed Charlotte's hand. "No one is ever going to understand you the way we do. You, Rose, and I share the same special gift. So what do you say, Charlotte? Are you willing to call Ireland your home?"

"And us, your family?" Rose looked at Charlotte with deep affection.

"I do think of all of you as my family," Charlotte spoke quietly. "I just never thought you would feel that way about me. I can't even imagine that you do. It's too wonderful." Charlotte looked as though she would cry.

"Now, don't start gettin' all mushy, or we'll all be bawlin' into our tea. We won't be havin' any of that," said Margaret as she gently wiped tears from her own eyes.

"It's settled then; she's staying!" Said Quinn.

Fiona got up from the table and uncorked a bottle of wine. After giving everyone a glass but Gracie (who had to make do with tea), Fiona caught her friend's eye, then raised her glass and smiled. "To Ireland, Quinn!"

Quinn raised her glass in response and smiled back at her friend. "To Ireland, Fee!"

"To Ireland!" Shouted everyone at the table as they raised their glasses in the air.

www.ingramcontent.com/pod-product-compliance
Lightning Source LLC
LaVergne TN
LVHW090535110826
845146LV00003B/1107

9798988442332